To Amelia-
Be like
Enjoy~ "Eric"
Deborah K Fontera

ERIC AND THE ENCHANTED LEAF

The First Adventure

ISBN 0-9753410-0-6

Library of Congress Control Number

2004104425

Key words: 1. insects-fiction   2. nature-fiction

Eric and the Enchanted Leaf: The First Adventure

Second edition

Published by Jade Enterprises

11807 S. Fairhollow Ln., Suite 106

Houston, TX 77043

dfrontiera@msn.com

Book layout by Emerald Phoenix Media
Cover design by Ira S. Van Scoyoc

Printed in Hong Kong

About the Author:

Deborah K. Frontiera was raised in Michigan's Upper Peninsula and still enjoys her summers there. She and her husband have raised four daughters. She has published fiction, non-fiction and poetry since 1985, the same year she began teaching kindergarten in Houston Independent School District. Besides writing and teaching, she does programs on writing for teachers, students and other writers.

More information and news about the release of Eric's next adventure, go to www.authorsden.com/deborahkfrontiera

About the Illustrator:

Korey Scott grew up in Richmond, TX. He graduated from B.F. Terry High School in 1995 and received his Bachelor of Fine Arts degree from the University of North Texas, Denton, TX, in 2002. He currently works for the University of North Texas in the counseling and testing department. *Eric and the Enchanted Leaf* is the first picture book he has illustrated. His goal is to illustrate children's books full time.

DEDICATION

To Islea Duncan for her encouragement to the author, And to Larry and Kevin Scott for their belief in their son's artistic talent. Special thanks to Rita of the American Book Cooperative for her help with this project.

Eric and the Enchanted Leaf: *The First Adventure*

Curiosity leads Eric to grab an unusual leaf as it floats by him. In a whirl of enchantment from Sophia, the sky fairy, Eric finds himself trapped the web of a spider he intended to squash. Join Eric on his first adventure as he gains a new perspective on some of nature's tiny creatures.

Eric slammed the screen door and jumped down the steps. He climbed into the tire swing. A funny feeling came over him.

A mosquito landed on his leg. He reached down and swatted it.

A fuzzy striped caterpillar crawled out of the grass and up the tree trunk. Eric watched it hump up, stretch out, and hump up again.

"Hey, caterpillar, what are you doing?" asked Eric.

The caterpillar stopped and turned, as if to look at the dark-eyed boy. A shiver went through Eric.

Another movement caught his eye. He got off the swing. Two

lines of ants marched up and down the tree and off into the

grass.

Eric followed the ants to the flower bed. Among the canna lilies, he found the ant hill. The trail of ants going into a hole in the grainy mound carried bits of something. Those coming out at the top set down grains of dirt.

Eric wondered what was inside. He reached for a stiff magnolia leaf and used it like a shovel to dig into the ant hill. Ants swarmed out of the nest. Eric dropped the leaf and jumped back.

"Wow!"

The ants returning from the tree touched others. One or two spread the news down the line. All the workers rushed to the damaged area.

One ant strayed from the path and blundered into a spider web stretched between two flower stems. It struggled to free itself. The web twitched and swayed. An orange garden spider moved toward it.

"Oh, no you don't, you mean old spider," Eric said. "Let that little ant go or I'll squash you!"

Before he could do anything, the spider wrapped up the ant.

Suddenly, an emerald green leaf floated past his nose. He snatched it out of the air.

A tingling sensation traveled through him. The sky, the earth, and the sunlight swirled around. Eric felt himself falling down, down, down.

"Aaaaahhhhh…"

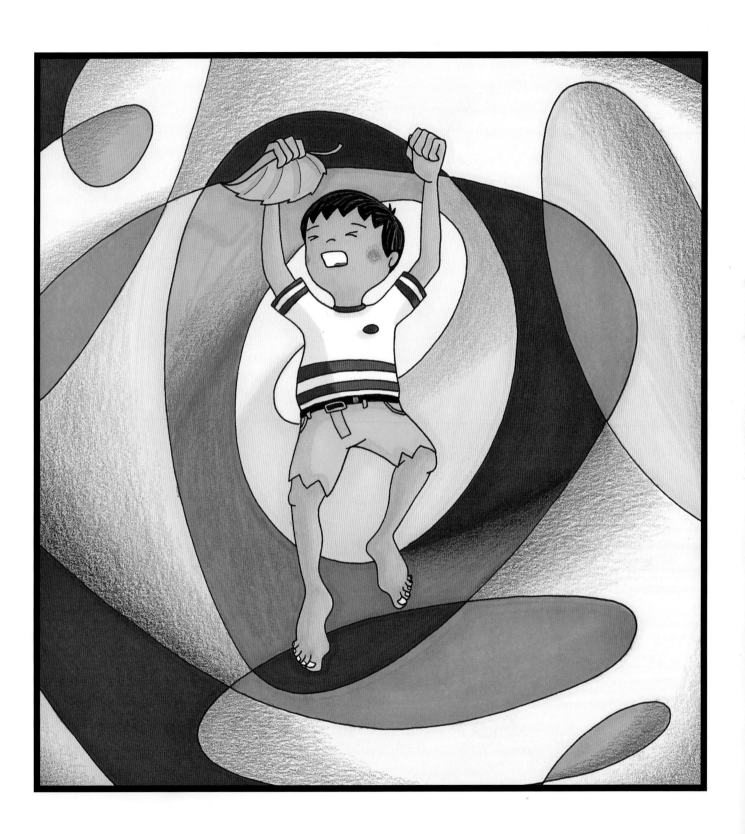

Eric landed in something, and stuck. He tried to sit up, but couldn't. Horror struck. The boy was tangled in the web! The spider, her body a pattern of orange and black, tapped the strands with her front legs.

"Now what was that you said about squashing me?" The spider poised herself to wrap Eric in her silk.

"Help!" yelled Eric.

"Wait, Madame Orange," a voice interrupted.

Eric turned his head and saw a lovely lady. Her face glowed like moonlight. Stars twinkled in her black hair. A breeze whispered through gauzy wings as blue as the sky. The green mist of new leaves covered her body and the fragrance of flowers filled the air. With a hand as brown as the garden dirt, she pulled Eric from the web.

Eric could only stare at her.

"Don't be afraid," she said.

"Who . . . who are you?"

"I am Sophia, the sky fairy. I was on the leaf that floated by you a moment ago. I transformed you."

"Why?" Eric asked.

"So you could satisfy your curiosity in a more meaningful way."

Eric wrinkled his eyes and nose. "Huh?"

"Your eyes are quick and you want to learn. Under the enchantment of the leaf, you will be able to understand the language of any living thing. All you have to do is hold the leaf and wish."

He turned and asked the spider, "Were you really going to kill me like a bug?"

The spider waved one leg at the sky fairy and said, "I wrap up and eat anything that blunders into my web. That's how I survive. It's my purpose in nature."

"I guess I never thought of that," Eric said.

The sky fairy smiled. "Do you want to ask Madame Orange anything else?"

"Yeah. Why don't you get stuck in your own web?"

"I have different kinds of silk. I make strong, thick silk for the frame of my web and use finer strands in between. Some is sticky, some isn't. I know which parts are which."

"Oh. Well, bye for now."

Eric walked away with Sophia. The spider began to repair her web.

The ant hill stood ahead. The part Eric had scooped away reminded him of a picture of a volcano. Dozens of ants crawled over the destruction, carrying away gravel and dirt. Soon, ants came out of the repaired entrance tunnel.

Eric looked at Sophia. "I really messed it up, didn't I? Did I kill any?"

"Not this time."

"Will they still let me in?"

"Why don't you ask?"

Eric approached one of the workers. He hung his head. "I'm sorry I messed up your home. I only wanted to see what was inside."

The ant cocked her head toward Eric. Then she touched him all over with her antennae. He smelled something strange but not unpleasant. There were no words, but thoughts came into his head.

"People, dogs, cats . . . so many things try to tear down our home. We must constantly rebuild."

"This is weird. How are you talking to me?"

"We communicate with smell and touch through our antennae."

Eric pointed at the tunnel. "Can I go in there?"

"Yes." The ant led him inside.

Eric hadn't gone far before he had to stop. "Hey, where did the light go?"

Several ants answered. "It's always dark underground. We don't need light. Our antennae tell us the way."

"But I can't see anything." Eric turned around and walked back to daylight.

His ant guide spoke again. "Our home is a maze of tunnels and rooms. In the deepest part lies our queen. We care for her and she lays all the eggs that become our sister workers."

"Why were so many of you going up the tree?"

The worker looked at the sky fairy.

"Come with me, Eric. I'll show you. The ants must get back to work."

Sophia flew him to a nest in the live oak. It was empty except for a dead baby cardinal.

Sophia explained. "The other birds flew away. This one was too weak. The ants carry away parts of the dead for food. Nothing is wasted."

Eric stared at the remains of the bird. "That isn't fair. It's mean."

"Nature is neither fair, nor unfair. Nature just is."

The sky fairy carried Eric back to the walk near his back door.

"Eric! Dinner time!" Eric recognized his mother's voice.

A giant shadow came over Eric and Sophia. The fairy grabbed his hand and pulled him into the grass. His mother's foot crashed down where they had been standing.

"Yeow!" cried Eric.

"You may keep the enchanted leaf," Sophia said. "Wish on it whenever you want to learn about the world around you."

"Really? Thanks!" Eric looked at the leaf again. "From now on, I'd better watch out where I'm walking."

The fairy shimmered into the grass. Eric stood on the walk, normal size, with the enchanted leaf in his hand. He spotted a crack under the side of the porch steps and hid the leaf for another day.

Then he started up the steps. "But I'm still going to swat mosquitoes."